WAFFLES THE CHICKEN
STANDS UP FOR OTHERS

KEN AND ASHLEY MATTHEWS

To Ashley, for always standing by my side.

-Ken

www.wafflesthechicken.com
email: info@wafflesthechicken.com
Rooster and Hen Publishing
Waffles the Chicken Stands Up For Others
Copyright © 2020 by Ken Matthews
All rights reserved.
ISBN: 978-1-953352-02-6

Waffles the Chicken loves everyone. If anyone is lonely, needs a playmate, or needs a friend, Waffles is happy to help.

He and Duck liked to play by the pond. They liked to kick a ball high in the air. If it landed in tall grass, Waffles went after it. If it landed in the water, Duck went after it. They played together so nicely.

But not everyone was so nice. Squirrel watched from the trees and shouted, "Hey, Duck! What's up with your hair? You look like a clown way down there!"

Duck's wings slumped. "I can't help how I look. I'm a crested duck and we all look this way."

Duck looked so sad, so Waffles said, "Don't worry about him, it's just farmyard fun. I'm sure Squirrel didn't mean to hurt anyone."

Maybe it was true, but Duck no longer wanted to play.

Waffles and Skunk liked to play hide and seek in the woods. With his red feathers, Waffles didn't hide well. With her white stripe, Skunk didn't hide well. It didn't matter. They played together so nicely.

But not everyone was so nice. Owl swooped down and shouted, "Hey, Skunk! My day was going so well! Leave this place before it starts to smell!"

Skunk frowned. "That's pretty rude. I only stink when I'm scared."

Skunk looked so sad, so Waffles said, "Don't worry about him, it's just farmyard fun. I'm sure that Owl didn't mean to hurt anyone."

Maybe it was true, but Skunk no longer wanted to play.

Waffles and Possum liked to play by the house. They liked to play treasure hunters. Waffles used his claws to search in the dirt. Possum used his tail to climb on the trash can. They played together so nicely.

But not everyone was so nice. Cat sat near the fence and shouted, "Hey, Possum, when did nature fail? It forgot to put any fur on your tail!"

Possum pouted. "I didn't choose a tail without fur, but it works well for holding me in place."

Possum looked so sad, so Waffles said, "Don't worry about her, it's just farmyard fun. I'm sure Cat didn't mean to hurt anyone."

Maybe it was true, but Possum no longer wanted to play.

Waffles saw his friend, Silkie the Chicken. Maybe she wanted to play.

"No," she said. "I don't think so. I have weird feathers on my feet."

"What?" Waffles said. "That's simply not true! No one would say that about you. Your furry feet are awfully neat!"

"Then why did you let Squirrel make
fun of the feathers on Duck's head?"

Waffles sat there and pondered.
Why did it matter to Silkie that
Squirrel made fun of Duck?

Waffles saw his friend, Pig. Maybe she wanted to play.

"No," Pig said. "I don't think so. A lot of animals think pigs smell."

"What?" Waffles said. "That's simply not true! No one would say that about you. You smell just fine!"

"But some people do, and you did nothing when Owl made fun of Skunk for her smell."

Waffles sat there and pondered. Why did it matter to Pig that Owl made fun of Skunk?

Waffles saw his friend, Sheep. Maybe he wanted to play.

"No," he said. "I don't think so. I was just sheared. Wouldn't that be weird?"

"What?" Waffles said. "That's simply not true! No one would say that about you. Even without your hair, you look great."

Waffles sat there and pondered. Why did it matter to Sheep that Cat made fun of Possum?

Waffles went back to the pond where he started his day.

"Duck, I don't understand. Why does anyone care that some animals say silly things in some farmyard fun?"

"You really don't get it?" Duck asked. "Farmyard fun is only fun when it's fun for everyone. When you sat there and watched, you said it was fine."

"I did not! I didn't say anything at all!"

"Sometimes saying nothing sure says a lot. You should stick up for your friends with all that you've got. You don't need to be bold or particularly brave to say stop the teasing and behave."

Maybe Duck was right.

The next day, Waffles and Goat played in the field. Waffles used his wings to jump and glide. Goat used her balance to dance on a log. They played together so nicely.

But not everyone was so nice. Fox watched from the grass and shouted, "Hey, Goat! What's up with your eyes? They're flat and they're strange like some kind of disguise."

Goat's head dropped. "My eyes are just different. There's nothing I can do."

Goat looked so sad, so Waffles said, "Stop it, Fox. That's not very nice. It's not farmyard fun if it's not fun for everyone."

Goat stood up and smiled. Fox went away, but Goat still wanted to play.

Thanks for reading!

If you love Waffles, there's plenty more! Join us at www.wafflesthechicken.com for FREE printable coloring pages and updates on new releases.

Don't forget to check out other books in the Waffles the Chicken series!

Made in the USA
Monee, IL
08 May 2021